Mr Nodd's A

by John Yeoman

illustrated by Quentin Blake

PUFFIN BOOKS

Some other books by John Yeoman and Quentin Blake

Picture books

MOUSE TROUBLE
THE DO-IT-YOURSELF HOUSE THAT JACK BUILT

In Young Puffin

FEATHERBRAINS

Poetry

THE FAMILY ALBUM

PUFFIN BOOKS

Published by the Penguin Group
Penguin Books Ltd, 27 Wrights Lane, London W8 5TZ, England
Penguin Books USA Inc., 375 Hudson Street, New York, New York 10014, USA
Penguin Books Australia Ltd, Ringwood, Victoria, Australia
Penguin Books Canada Ltd, 10 Alcorn Avenue, Toronto, Ontario, Canada M4V 3B2
Penguin Books (NZ) Ltd, 182–190 Wairau Road, Auckland 10, New Zealand

Penguin Books Ltd, Registered Offices: Harmondsworth, Middlesex, England

First published by Hamish Hamilton Ltd 1995
Published in Puffin Books 1997
1 3 5 7 9 10 8 6 4 2

Mr Nodd loved doing woodwork. He had a fine set of tools, and he was very proud of them. The trouble was, he was running out of ideas for things to make.

He still had a lot of wood left. "I know," said Mr Nodd; "I'll build a boat in the garden!"

"I hope your father knows what he's doing," said Mrs Nodd.

With the help of his older sons he built a boat so enormous that it almost touched the garden walls.

His wife looked out of the bedroom window. "It's very nice," she said, "but isn't it a bit big? How are you going to get it out of the garden?"

Mr Nodd hadn't thought of that.

Later, when they sat down to their tea, Mr Nodd was looking very glum.

"You're not knocking the garden wall down," said Mrs Nodd.

"And you mustn't break up the boat," said Ham.

Just then Shem put on the television. The weather-lady was saying that there could be serious floods within the next two days.

"That's it!" cried Mr Nodd, leaping up: "I'll turn it into an ark. And then it can float over the wall."

Ham and Shem thought that this was a marvellous idea.

"I don't know where I'm going to hang my washing," said Mrs Nodd.

"But you can't have an ark without animals. In pairs," said Ham.

"Well, we've got two hamsters and two cats," said Shem, "and two goldfish and two budgies."

"And we could borrow some more," said Ham.

"Very well, then," said Mrs Nodd, "but no stick insects."

The next day the boys went round to their friends and borrowed two rabbits, two grass snakes, two white mice, and two ducks. By a stroke of luck two stray mongrels followed them home.

That evening Mrs Nodd collected up all their wooden cups and plates and cutlery, and the boys got down to making piles of sandwiches.

"We'd better get a move on," said Mr Nodd; "the rain might come quite suddenly. You know, I think we ought to spend the night in the ark."

They all agreed. So they passed the sandwiches and the beds and the guitars, and the bits and pieces that Mrs Nodd had packed, out of the bedroom window and on to the ark.

"Don't you think it's cosy?" said Mr Nodd, lighting the storm lamp.

"Wouldn't it be better with windows?"
asked Mrs Nodd.

"That'd be silly," he replied. "What good are wooden windows?"

They were all just settling down for the evening when they heard a knock at the door.

"I'll see who it is," said Ham.

Imagine their surprise when they saw two large sheep standing there.

"Better let them in," said Mrs Nodd.
"There's still room. Just."

"I wonder how they got to know about it," said Shem.

"You'd be surprised at the gossip that goes on in the supermarket," said his mother.

"Pull the gangplank up and bar the door now, boys," said Mr Nodd. "We could be afloat soon."

The newcomers made themselves comfortable.

"I can't just sit here doing nothing," said Mrs Nodd; "this could last quite a while."

"Forty days and forty nights usually," said Mr Nodd.

"The weather-lady said until Wednesday," said Shem.

"All the same, I'm getting on with making the decorations for next Christmas," said Mrs Nodd. "If anyone wants to help, they're welcome."

Everyone volunteered. The light wasn't very good, and the decorations were rather rough and ready. But they fascinated the animals and kept them quiet.

Finally, tired and contented, they all crept under their hinged blankets and went to sleep.

The gangway was lowered, and the Nodd family and
the animals, all blinking in the light, came out on deck
to greet their guests.

"The floods have gone down, then?" said Mr Nodd.

The children looked blank.

Mrs Nodd peered around. "You know," she said,
"I don't think we've had much more than a
heavy downpour."

Mr Nodd looked very disappointed.

"That's a terrific disco you've built there, Mr Nodd,"
said one little girl.

"Really?" he said, brightening up. "Oh, thank you."

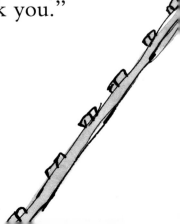

"Now that's an idea, Dad," said Shem. "It could be ages before the next flood, and mum doesn't want you to knock the garden wall down ..."

"... and you don't want to break the ark up," said Ham. "So couldn't we use it once a week for dancing?"

"Please, Mr Nodd," they all shouted.

Mrs Nodd looked at her husband. "It does seem a shame to waste it," she said, "and we did have such a good time. Why not give it a try?"

So Mr Nodd got out his toolkit and ran an electric cable from the house so that he could put up coloured lights all round the cabin. Then he set up the boys' sound system and fitted the place out like a real disco.

It was brilliant.

And, do you know, every Saturday evening when Ham and Shem and little Japhet let down the gangway and open the door, there's always a long queue of eager children waiting.

And a few pairs of animals.